Words to Know Before You Read

backpack

calculator

electricity

forgetful

hamper

neglected

refrigerator

remember

rummaged

wasting

www.rourkeeducationalmedia.com

Edited by Precious McKenzie
Illustrated by Ed Myer
Art Direction and Page Layout by Renee Brady

Library of Congress PCN Data

Money Down the Drain / Kyla Steinkraus
ISBN 978-1-61810-196-9 (hard cover) (alk. paper)
ISBN 978-1-61810-329-1 (soft cover)
Library of Congress Control Number: 2012936797

Rourke Educational Media
Printed in China, Artwood Press Limited,
   Shenzhen, China

rourkeeducationalmedia.com

customerservice@rourkeeducationalmedia.com • PO Box 643328 Vero Beach, Florida 32964

Money $ $ $
Down the Drain

By Kyla Steinkraus
Illustrated by Ed Myer

Wendy Wilson was a forgetful girl.

At school, she always forgot her calculator for math class.

Her backpack often spent the night on the bus.

At home, Wendy neglected to put her dirty clothes in the hamper. And she usually forgot to put her dirty dishes in the sink.

She didn't try to forget. She just didn't remember.

The one thing Wendy always, for sure, 100% of the time, forgot to do was save electricity.

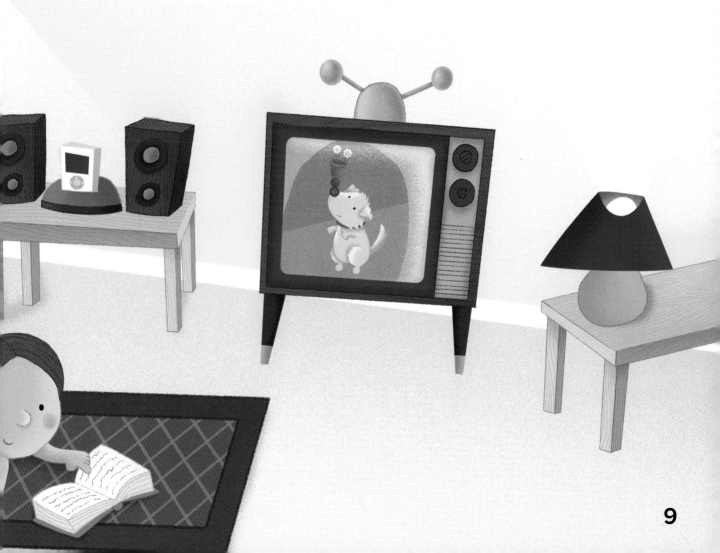

She always left her bedroom light on. In fact, Wendy left a trail of lights on throughout the house.

Whenever she felt the least bit chilly, she turned the heat all the way up.

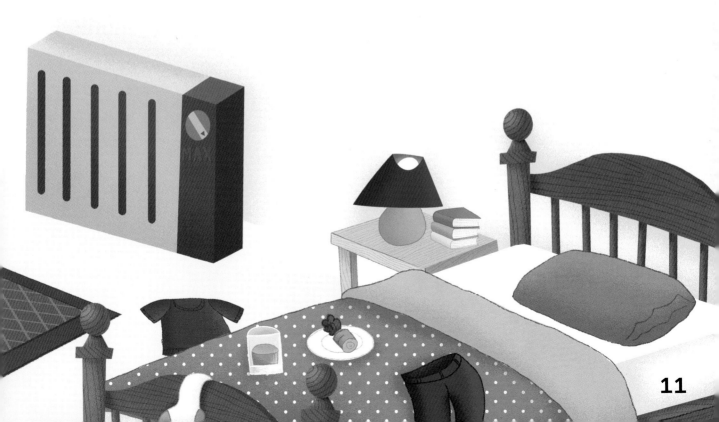

"Please just get a sweater," Mom said, wiping sweat from her forehead.

"I'm sorry!" Wendy said. She meant it, but then she forgot.

When Wendy was hungry, she rummaged through the refrigerator for a glass of milk and a slice of cheese. She didn't notice when she left the refrigerator door wide open.

Wendy sat on the couch to watch her favorite cartoon. When it was over, she went outside to play, not realizing that the TV was still on.

When she came back inside, Mom was waiting. "Wendy, did you know that wasting electricity is like tossing money down the drain?"

Wendy imagined wads and wads of dollar bills clogging her bathtub drain.

Mom said, "We have to pay money for all the electricity that brightens our rooms, heats our house, and keeps our food fresh."

Wendy thought for a minute. "Even when I am not in the room, the electricity is still running?" she asked. Mom nodded. *Wendy finally got it!* Mom thought.

Wendy dashed to her room. She started to empty her piggy bank down the drain.

"No, stop!" yelled Mom. "What are you doing?"

"I am putting my money down the drain to pay for the electricity," Wendy said.

"That is just a figure of speech. It means we are wasting money," Mom said. "But I want to help," said Wendy.

Mom hugged Wendy. "Saving electricity is a great place to start."

After Reading Activities

You and the Story...

What are some of the ways Wendy was forgetful?

How did Wendy waste electricity?

What did Wendy decide to do to help her remember to save electricity?

What could you do to save electricity?

Words You Know Now...

Write four sentences using three of the words below in each sentence. You can reuse words.

backpack	neglected
calculator	refrigerator
electricity	remember
forgetful	rummaged
hamper	wasting

You Could...Teach Your Family How to Save Electricity

Have a family meeting where you explain how electricity is wasted, such as:

- Turn lights off when you leave a room.
- Turn off the TV when you're done.
- Shut the fridge door after every use.
- Keep hot showers short.
- Put on a sweater instead of turning up the heat.

Create ways to help family members remember to save electricity, such as:

- Put post it notes next to light switches.
- Use a code word to remind each other, such as "Lights!"
- Create a reward account with the money your family saves. Use it to play miniature golf or go bowling together.

About the Author

Kyla Steinkraus lives in Tampa, Florida with her husband and two kids. She tries to save electricity whenever she can. Her family likes to go to a restaurant with the money they save from remembering to turn off the lights.

Ask The Author!
www.rem4students.com

About the Illustrator

Ed Myer is a Manchester-born illustrator now living in London. After growing up in an artistic household, Ed studied ceramics at university but always continued drawing pictures. As well as illustration, Ed likes traveling, playing computer games, and walking little Ted (his Jack Russell).